This book belongs to:

Digital art by Callaway Animation Studios under the direction of David Kirk in collaboration
with Nelvana Limited.

This book is based on the TV episode "Flower Power," written by Michael Stokes, from the animated TV
series *Miss Spider's Sunny Patch Friends* on Nick Jr., a Nelvana Limited/Absolute Pictures Limited
co-production in association with Callaway Arts & Entertainment,
based on the Miss Spider books by David Kirk.

Nicholas Callaway, President and Publisher
Cathy Ferrara, Managing Editor and Production Director
Toshiya Masuda, Art Director • Nelson Gómez, Director of Digital Services
Joya Rajadhyaksha, Associate Editor • Amy Cloud, Associate Editor
Raphael Shea, Senior Designer • Krupa Jhaveri, Designer
Bill Burg, Digital Artist • Christina Pagano, Digital Artist • Mary Boyer, Digital Artist

Special thanks to the Nelvana staff, including Doug Murphy, Scott Dyer, Tracy Ewing, Pam Lehn,
Tonya Lindo, Mark Picard, Jane Sobol, Luis Lopez, Eric Pentz, and Georgina Robinson.

Library of Congress Cataloging-in-Publication Data available upon request.

Distributed in the United States by Viking Children's Books.

Callaway Arts & Entertainment, its Callaway logotype,
and Callaway & Kirk Company LLC are trademarks.

ISBN 978-0-448-44504-5

Visit Callaway Arts & Entertainment at www.callaway.com

10 9 8 7 6 5 4 3 2 1   07 08 09 10

First edition, January 2007

Printed in China

Miss Spider, Eunice Earwig, and their children were picnicking at the Taddy Puddle.

Li'l Sis Earwig and Honey Bee splashed around with Felix Frog.

"HELP! The pondscum monster is going to to eat us!" they giggled.

"Sunny Patch Superheroes to the rescue!" yelled Dragon as he, Squirt, and Shimmer flew overhead. The threesome swooped down and grabbed Li'l Sis and Honey.

"You little bugs should really be more careful," Shimmer said as she put Honey on the ground.

"Hey, don't call us little!" Honey squeaked in protest.

"Yeah," agreed Li'l Sis, "we don't need anybuggy to look after us."

Just then, Miss Spider crawled over. "Everybuggy pair up—big buggies with little buggies!"

"Good idea," Eunice agreed. "You look out for your buddy and your buddy will look out for you."

The kids thought buddying up was for babies. But they did as their mothers told them and flew off to play in the meadow.

"This time *we* want to be superheroes," demanded Li'l Sis.

"But what superpowers do you little bugs have?" Dragon asked.

"We have flower power!" Honey announced proudly.

"Yeah! We can crawl into tiny flowers where big bugs can't go," added Li'l Sis.

Dragon, Shimmer, and Squirt laughed. Flower power?

"Come on, Li'l Sis," Honey said angrily, "let's go play flower power by ourselves."

Remembering their buddy system, Felix started to go after them, but Shimmer stopped him. "They'll be fine," she said.

Honey and Li'l Sis took turns playing hide and seek. Li'l Sis hid in a big honeysuckle blossom. But while she was waiting to be found, she fell asleep.

"Li'l Sis, where are you?" called Honey.

"Time to eat!" Miss Spider announced just as Squirt, Shimmer, Dragon, and Felix arrived. "Where are the others?"

"Li'l Sis and Honey went off by themselves," Squirt said.

"But you were supposed to buddy up!" Eunice said.

Just then, Honey flew over. "I can't find Li'l Sis!" she cried.

Everybuggy searched for Li'l Sis, but they could find no sign of her!

"She was my buddy," Shimmer said sadly. "I shouldn't have left her alone."

"We'll find her," Miss Spider soothed.

Miss Spider told the bugs to sit tight while she went for help.

"If we were real superheroes," Dragon said glumly, "we could find her."

Just then, the bugs heard a feeble cry.

"Help! Somebuggy help me!"

"That's Li'l Sis!" Honey cried. "It sounds like she's in the honeysuckle bush!"

"Shimmer," Squirt said, "your superpower heat sensors can find her!"

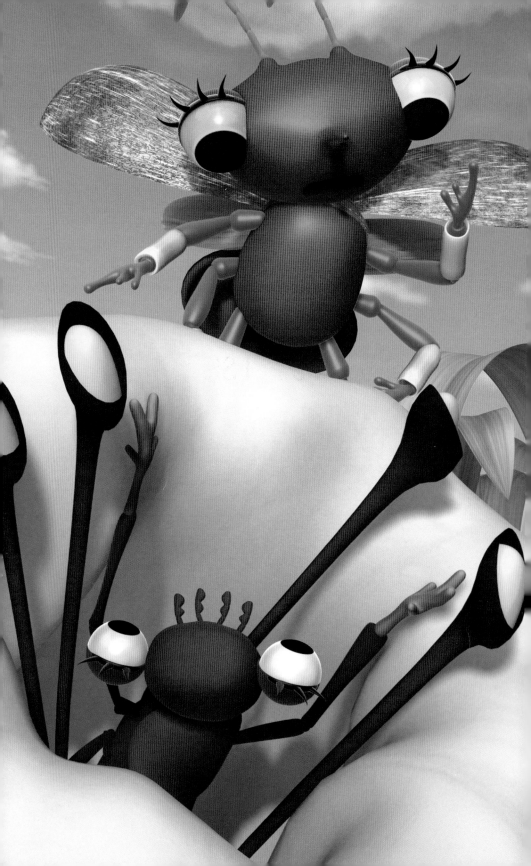

Shimmer took a deep breath and hovered above the bush. She felt her heat sensors twitch this way and that. Finally, she flew to the biggest blossom, and inside was Li'l Sis.

"I'm stuck in some nectar!" she cried.

"I can't get her out!" Shimmer called as she pulled and tugged at Li'l Sis.

"I think we need your flower power!" Shimmer told Honey.

They tied a web thread around Honey and lowered her into the flower. She grabbed Li'l Sis, while the others tugged at the end of the thread.

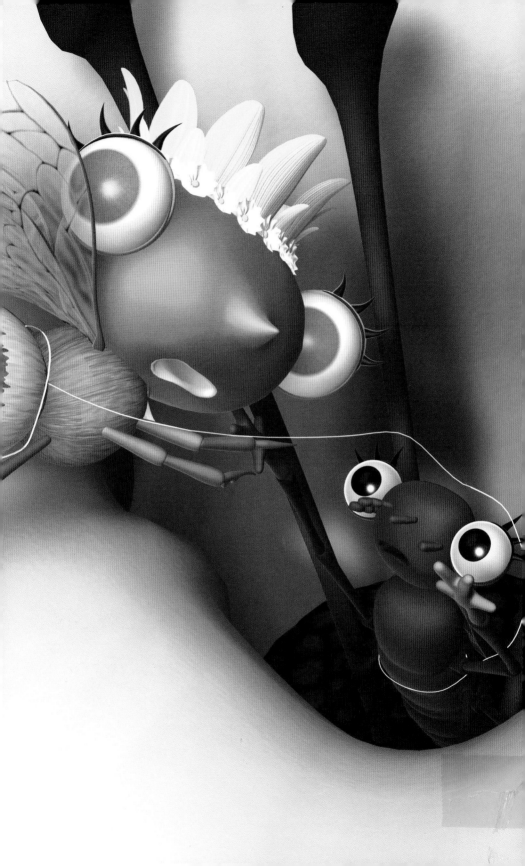

Finally, they plucked the little earwig free of the sticky flower. Miss Spider and Eunice crawled over.

"My baby!" Eunice squealed, hugging Li'l Sis.

"I'm so proud of the way you kids came through," beamed Miss Spider.

"We were wrong," Squirt admitted to Honey. "Flower power is actually pretty cool."

"And you and Li'l Sis are real superheroes," Dragon added.

"Forget superheroes," Shimmer announced. "From now on, we're the Sunny Patch Super-Buddies!"